Fair or Unfair?

CIVIC VIRTUES

Gillian Clifton

CIVICS FOR THE REAL WORLD™

Rosen Classroom™

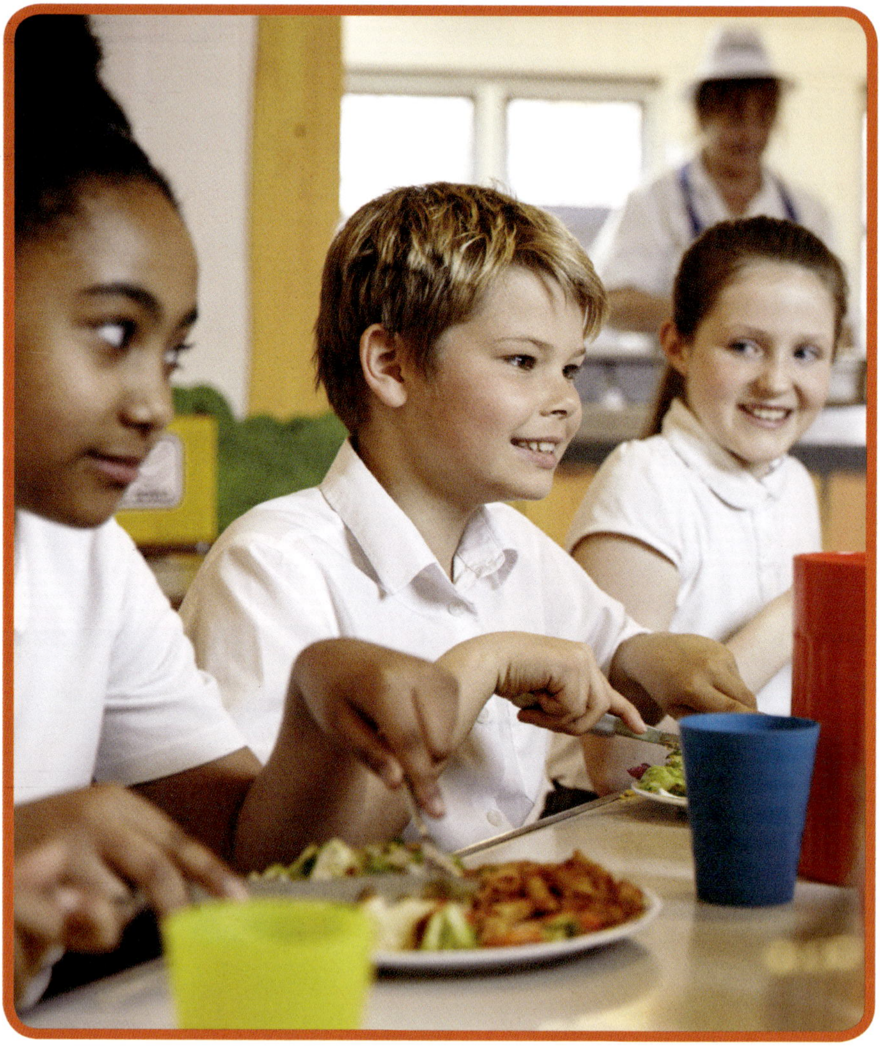

This is my lunch table.

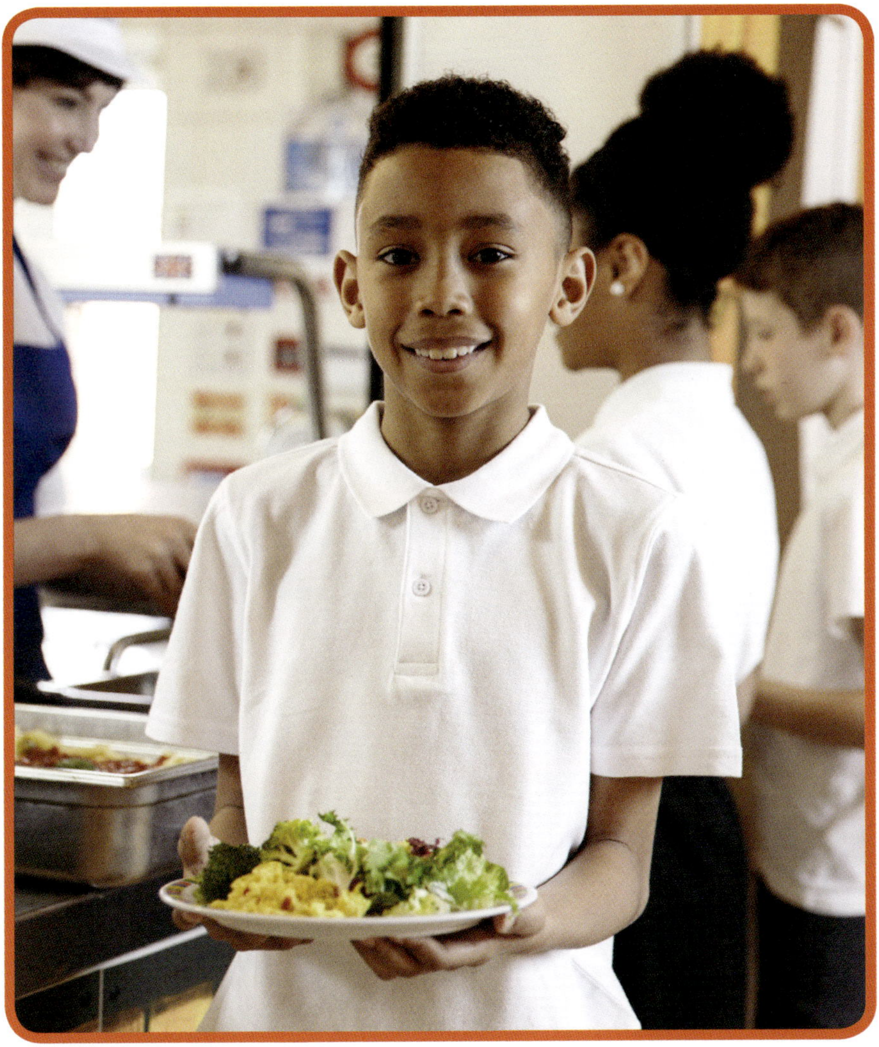

Ty wants to sit.

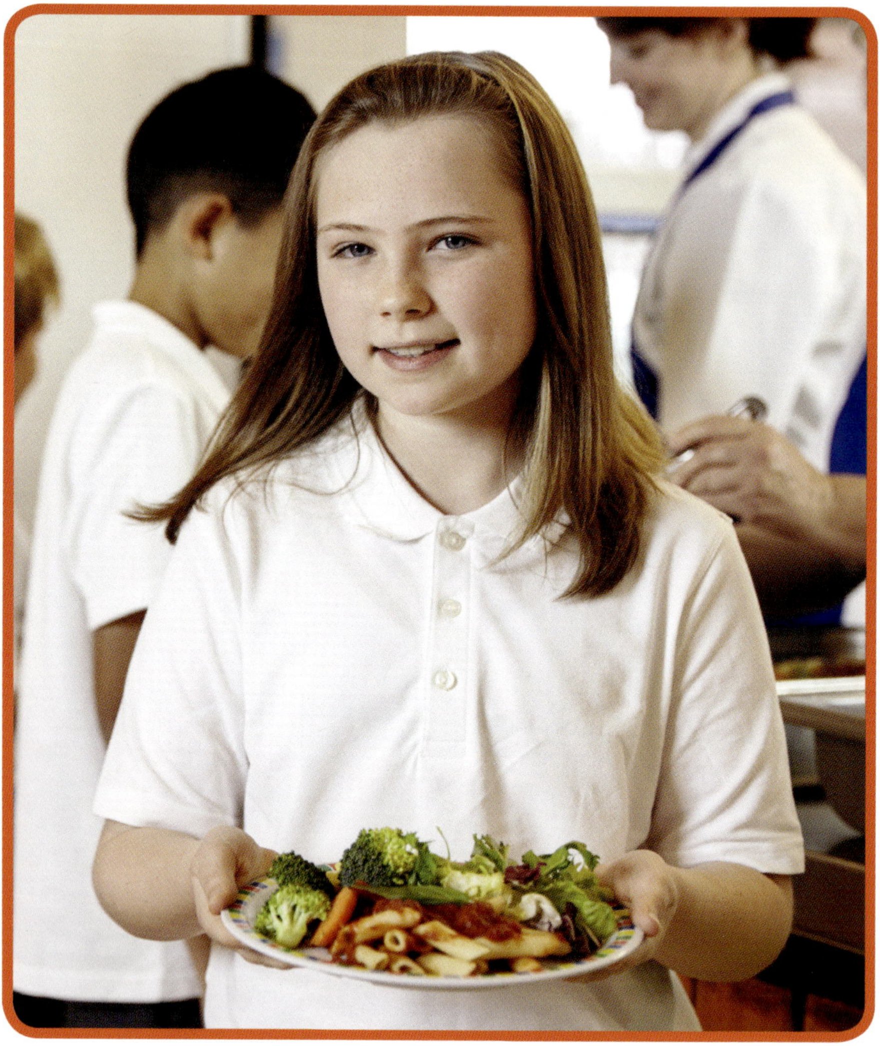

Jen says no.

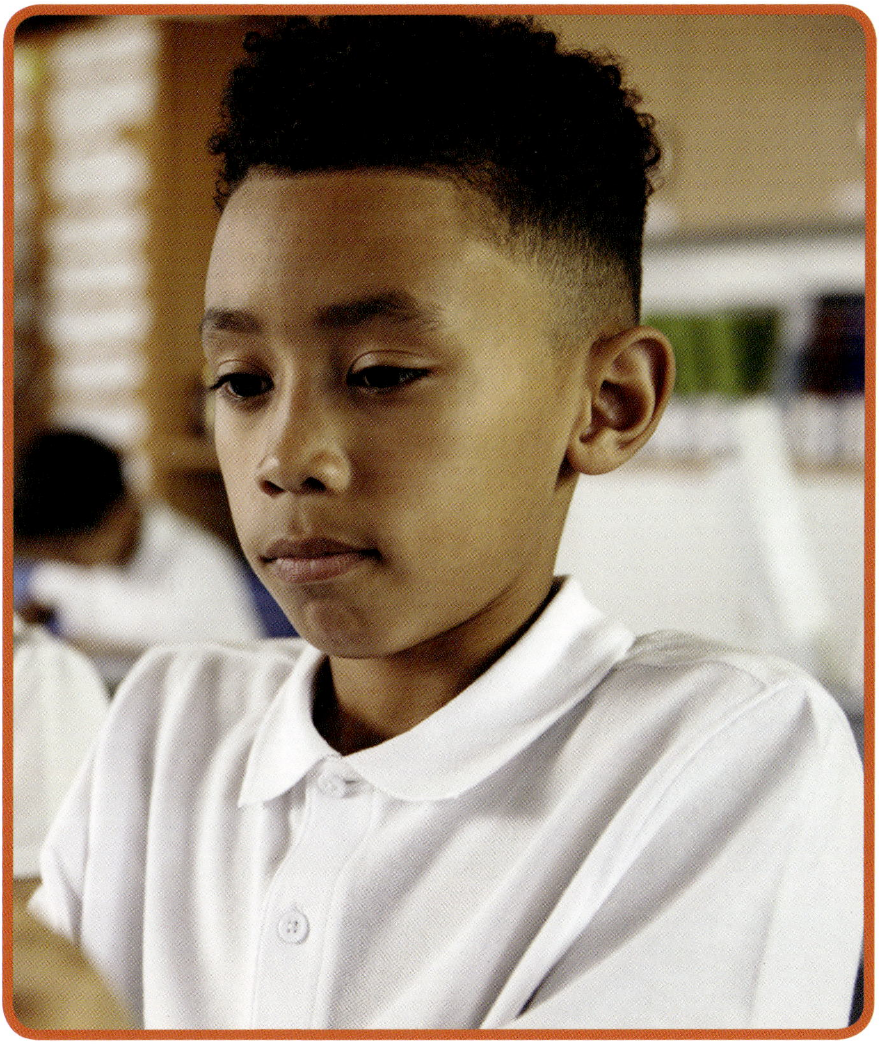

That is not fair!

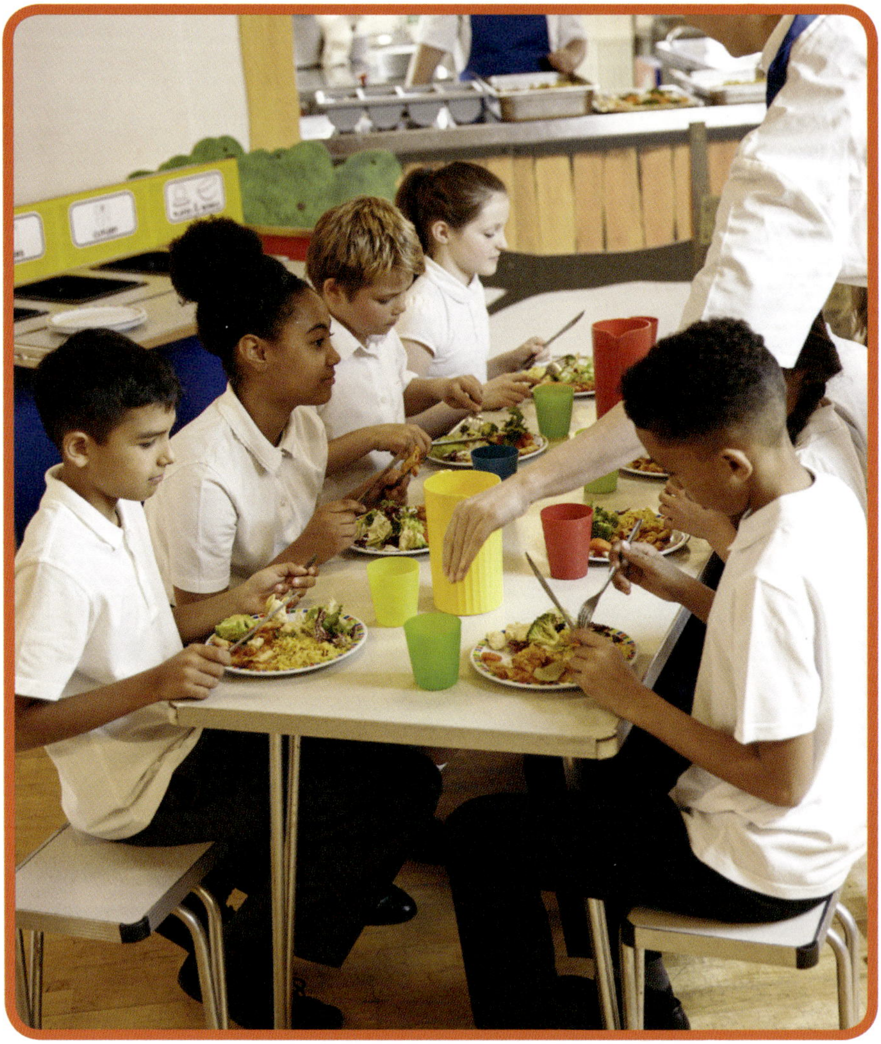

I let Ty sit with us.

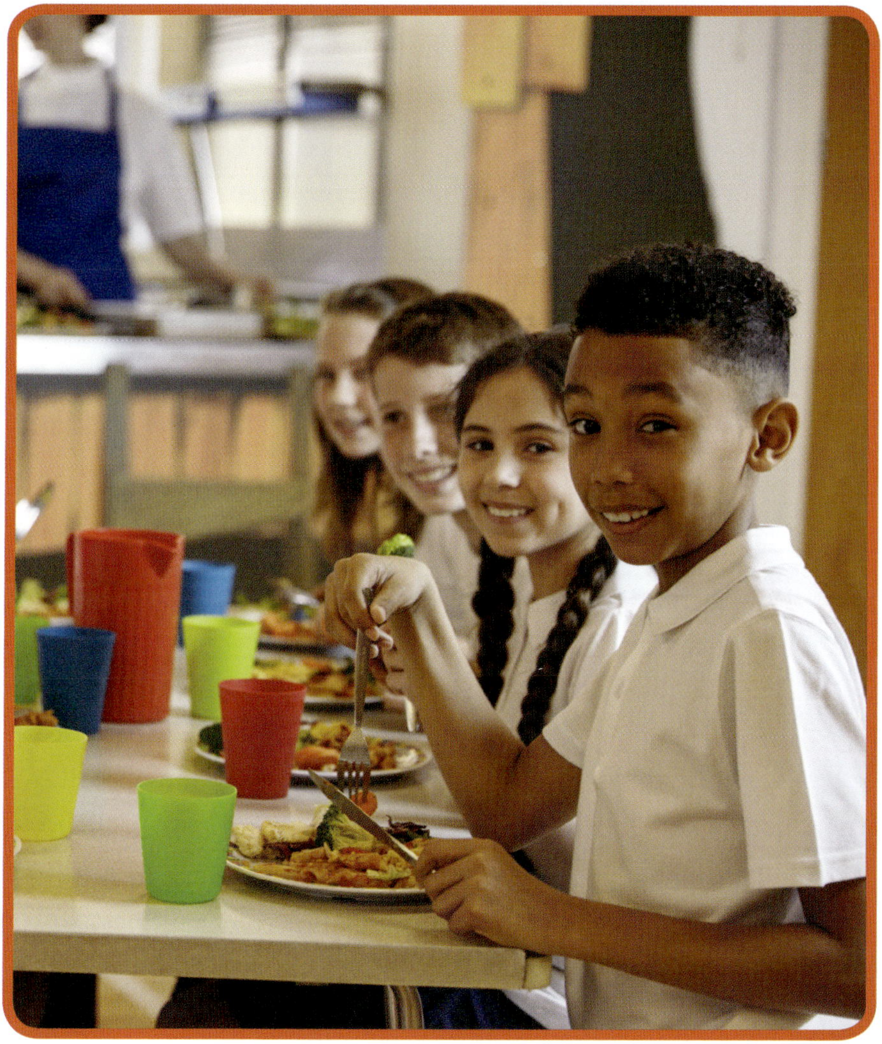

That is fair and kind.

WORDS TO KNOW

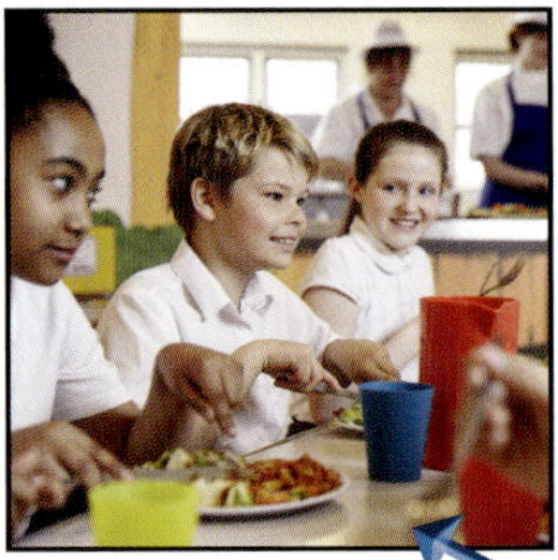

table